Whispers Through the Forest

With warmest wishes,
Heather Russell-Kay.
☺ xxx

Heather Russell-Kay

Dedicated to everyone who wakes each day to fight the same battles as the day before. To those who know that not every fairy tale is perfect but still believe in finding a little bit of magic along the way. And to anyone who happens to stumble across this book.

Thank you for being here and coming along on this adventure with me.

"I am out with lanterns, looking for myself."

-Emily Dickinson

Contents

Dorma's Beauty

Many, many years ago, a noble King and Queen lived in a magnificent castle deep within the wild forests of Somnum. They possessed everything they desired: wealth, land, and happiness. Yet one thing was missing from their lives: a child.

After many seasons, their wishes were eventually granted, and they became devoted parents to a beautiful baby girl named Dorma. In celebration, they invited people from all across the land to a great feast. And before its conclusion, magical gifts were bestowed upon the infant princess: virtue, beauty, and wealth.

But the most important gift had not been presented—the gift of health.

Dorma grew more and more beautiful with each passing day, and her kindness shone brightly like a beacon of light. Everyone who met her adored her, and she soon became the talk of the kingdom.

Nothing seemed able to hinder her until the day of her fifteenth birthday, when she was suddenly submerged by a suffocating sleepiness.

She retired to her bed, her family convinced that the excitement of the day had simply overwhelmed her.

Yet the drowsiness persisted, and Dorma could manage little more than to sit at her window for a few moments a day before being forced back to the confines of her bed.

***

Days passed, and talk of over-excitement or a lingering cold faded. In their place, whispered suspicions crept into the castle's corners. Perhaps she was simply being lazy?

Of course, the finest doctors in the land were summoned to examine her, who now could not even muster up the energy to lift herself from her bed. Her body betrayed her, yet, upon inspection, none of the physicians could discover a cause.

After every examination, from her bed, Dorma heard them muttering, even chuckling to themselves. A young girl who doesn't wish to do her chores, they said. Not uncommon, they said—fifteen-year-olds can be difficult. Or, as some others suggested, perhaps she's merely being dramatic. A touch of tiredness, and she claims she cannot move…

The doctors always left with a lightness of tone in their voices and a shake of their heads.

The castle's suspicions, no longer whispered, grew louder.

And Dorma, with her tears, a cold river streaming down her cheeks, continued to sleep.

Her parents, exasperated by her weakness and prolonged inactivity, began to grow cold towards her.

And still Dorma slept, as the shadow of sadness enveloped her.

***

Exactly one year after Dorma's fifteenth birthday, her parents resolved to find a young prince to marry their daughter. At least then the castle's future would be secure.

Many princes came, each wrenching fresh tears of despair from Dorma's eyes as they mocked her silently with their amused glances. They all saw the silly little girl trying to gain attention. None would listen when she tried to explain her endless tiredness.

One by one, they departed, resigned to the fact that they would not wed the sleeping beauty. They carried away rumours instead, for though her parents longed for her marriage, even they would not force their weeping daughter into such misery.

After each rejection, Dorma sank further beneath the heavy folds of darkness, each breath a struggle against its suffocating hold.

***

One sunny day, a handsome prince happened to pass the castle. Thirsty, he enquired whether he might drink from the spring outside the great doors.

The guards readily agreed. At that same moment, the elegant Queen, pondering her daughter's fate, crossed the courtyard. Her eyes fell upon the young gentleman, and she hurried over. Gently, she suggested he meet her daughter—she could not let the chance slip by.

Intrigued, and having long heard whispers of Dorma's beauty, he agreed. He was curious too, for no one had seen her in many months, and the rumours of her laziness lingered.

Following the Queen, he moved swiftly through the castle. Entering the chamber, he was greeted by the sight of Dorma. Her pale, pretty head resting upon her soft pillows, sleeping yet another day that felt to her like a hundred years.

A soft cough escaped him. Dorma's eyes fluttered slowly open, and her heart sank: yet another prince had come to mock her.

"Please leave," she whispered. "I know what you all think. But none see how I am a prisoner to sleep—destined to be alone, shut away from the world as it moves on without me."

But this prince did not chuckle. He did not shake his head, nor raise his brows in disbelief. Instead, he sat by her bed, lightly took her hand, and gazed into her tear-filled eyes.

"What do you want?" he asked softly.

A terrible understanding rolled through him. He knew this kind of sleep. He had watched it consume someone he once loved.

"I want to be free of this prison," she breathed. "I want to stand among the living again. But most of all… I want to be believed."

His fingers curled around hers; not hard, but with a quiet vow in it.

A beat.

A beat that felt like centuries.

Then three words left him, fragile, but unshakable, and Dorma's heart, for the first time in years, remembered how to hope.

"I believe you."

Fragile Kingdoms

Once upon a time, in a small cottage nestled sleepily among gently rolling hills and quiet meadows, there lived a man whose heart was filled with vibrancy and light, and his loving wife, whose very presence wrapped everyone in warmth. They had a beautiful daughter, Amare, who was curious and kind. For many years, they lived merrily together, enjoying a summer of harmonious happiness.

But as one winter crept silently from the shadows, a darkness slipped quietly into their home.

The nights grew longer, and the wife grew colder.

She grew paler, until her strength ebbed slowly away, leaving only a faint echo of her once fierce light.

***

On a bleak November evening, she gently called Amare to her bedside. With thin, frail hands, she clasped her daughter's, trying to pour all her love into her.

Her voice trembled as she whispered, "No matter where I go, I will always be with you—watching over you, protecting you from harm. Please, do not be afraid… I love you."

With these last murmured words, her eyelids fluttered like weary curtains, and a soft, eternal blanket settled over her. Amare sat rigid in the still silence, the house so deathly quiet that the tick of the clock echoed sharply through the room.

Tick…

Tick…

Tick…

The clock's steady beat, carrying on with indifferent rhythm, only cut the loss deeper.

Amare felt herself gasping for breath, her lungs shallow, her mind fixated on the sound.

Tick…

Tick…

Tick…

With each steady beat, her heart grew more hollow. The fragile light she carried flickered and dimmed as she longed to remain in this moment, rather than face the world without her mother's loving presence.

But no wish could halt time.

***

Days blurred into weeks, weeks into months. Soon, a year had passed, and spring's first blossoms unfurled, bringing the faintest promise of hope.

However, her father, colder and more distant since their light had passed into the otherworld, returned—and not alone. With him came a new wife, elegant and poised, and her two daughters, delicate as snowdrops with hair that gleamed like moonlight. Yet within, their frozen hearts were sharp and ruthless.

At first, their cruelty was subtle: small thefts of Amare's clothing, softly spoken but stern commands, careful smiles masking malicious minds. Then came the endless chores: scrubbing, sweeping, tending. Amare's hands grew raw, her body ached from dawn till dusk. Nights were worse, as she lay on the hard wooden floor, loneliness pressing down like a slow drift of leaves in a hollow forest.

Even so, in the miserable, suffocating fog that seemed to surround her and her new life, she found her way to her mother's grave each day. Kneeling in the damp grass, tracing moss-softened letters with trembling fingers, she held fast to the memory of her mother's love—a dim but steady light she clung to.

***

One particularly grey, despondent afternoon, as she sat quietly by her mother's resting place, heaven's tears whispered against the earth. A small white bird appeared, delicate as a feather and as small as a petal. It alighted upon the headstone and met her gaze with kind, thoughtful eyes.

"Oh," she whispered to her new companion, "how I wish to escape this life."

The bird waited, then opened its tiny beak and began to sing. It was a song heavy with sorrow, yet carrying the promise of hope.

Enchanted, Amare rose and followed it for what seemed like miles: through thyme-scented meadows, forests where sunlight danced, and thick bracken that clawed at her arms, until they opened out to reveal a small clearing. There, snug in the centre, stood a little cottage with a thatched roof, a white picket fence, and roses nodding merrily in the breeze.

The bird took flight with a cheerful chirp, leaving her alone in the sanctuary. Somehow, she knew—it was meant for her.

***

Days passed in quiet comfort, filled with serenity and peace. Each morning, she received greetings from her elderly neighbour, who would peek her head over the rose bushes. Each afternoon, she spoke quietly to the little bird, who would return to perch on the windowsill.

Soon, the cottage filled with the fragrance of homemade bread and biscuits, and flowers blossomed beautifully under her care. Her laughter returned to tenderly fill the air.

But after she had settled into this cosy and comforting routine, small troubles began: wallpaper curled from the walls, taps dripped, window hinges groaned to a tune only they knew. She mended each fault diligently, only to see, in disbelief, new flaws replacing them quicker than she could repair them.

***

Every day, more troubles peeked out their mischievous noses. The doorknobs fell off, paint peeled, pipes leaked, floorboards lifted, and the wallpaper kept curling away from the walls.

"It's a cosy place," smiled the old neighbour wistfully one day, as Amare desperately tried to argue the roses into submission as they attacked her viciously with their tiny, thorny fingers. "I'd give anything to live there."

Amare shook her head in despair as she simultaneously let out another yelp of pain as a thorn deeply dug mercilessly into her finger. "Can't you see what it's like? It's terrible! No matter what I do, it keeps coming apart!"

The woman, bemused, reassured her kindly. "Don't worry, dear. All homes have their flaws—a few small problems. We must accept them, as we do ourselves. I knew it was right for you the moment I saw you both together."

A few small problems? Amare thought bitterly. From the outside, perhaps. But she saw the truth in every uneven floorboard and curling corner: the house was flawed, stubborn… and perhaps even hated her.

She did not like it. She did not want it.

But she had nowhere else to go. So each day she pressed on—fixing leaks, hammering floorboards, and pasting wallpaper back onto the walls over and over and over again.

Her distress grew until the whole house consumed her. She began to weep throughout the day and sleep restlessly throughout the night. For even when she was tucked up in bed, she could hear the house creaking, groaning, growling. And in the moments where she managed to snatch some sleep, it was filled with nightmares of the roses coming alive and clutching at her with their sharp, pointy, little fingers; the house's walls falling off and letting the wind violently dart through; and the pathway disappearing into an unknown abyss, preventing her from ever leaving.

She was consistently startled awake by a new, alarming noise the house was making. How could anyone live like this?

The whole time, the house seemed to revel in its troublesome behaviour, like a child having a continuous roguish tantrum, but one that never needed to rest.

***

At last, one evening, when the wallpaper curled and fell into her hands for the thousandth time, something inside her broke.

She seized her coat and fled, slamming the door behind her as the cold wind swept her along the path and away from the never-ending nightmare.

She ran and ran, without knowing where she was going or what she was doing. Yet, impossibly, after a few short minutes, there it stood in front of her—the cottage, as beautiful as when she first saw it.

Confused, she turned back in the opposite direction. She shook her head to try to clear the labyrinth of confusion that it had become. She was sure she had not looped around on herself during her determination to escape the menacing abode. But after what seemed a mile of careful trudging along the path to ensure no accidental detours, the familiar cottage's thatched roof rose once more before her, innocent among its roses.

It was impossible. She knew she had not gone in circles. Dread filled the pit of her stomach. The cottage was doing this. It was trapping her here.

Infuriated, she turned around again and started in the direction of the village, only to see the small bird reappear in front of her, singing its hopeful tune and urging her return. Anger flared. None of this would have happened if it weren't for this small starling. She stomped on.

"I'm leaving!" she cried. "And you can't stop me!"

Glancing to the side, she saw her elderly next-door neighbour in a bright blue pinafore, waving happily to her from her garden.

Amare ignored her.

She ignored the bird.

She ignored the pull of the house tugging at her core.

She marched swiftly through the brambles, through the forest and through the meadows, towards her mother's grave, for that was the only place she felt she had left to go to.

Upon arriving, the bird perched familiarly on the headstone, but this time the sun was peeking out from behind the clouds, as though welcoming her home for a short visit.

Tears began to softly fall as her mind travelled back to a time long ago, when she lived in a home full of happiness and merriment with her mother and father. She smiled, even as her heart longed to return to those precious moments.

But with them came memories of her stepmother and stepsisters. In some ways, life had been easier: she just did what she was told back then. But it had been hard, and it had not been hers. It was a life for the new family her father had pieced together.

Resting her fingers lightly beside her feathered leader, she felt herself softening to the wilful pull of the house.

Deep down, he knew the truth: the house was hers. Troubled and flawed, yes, but part of her. She could not leave it behind, whether she wished to or not. They were entwined like honeysuckle and ivy.

With a heavy sigh, she pushed herself up and trekked back through the meadows, through the forests and through the brambles.

The cottage, honest and unyielding, with its curling wallpaper and dripping taps, was waiting for her return. It was imperfect, but it was hers. Breathing in the scent of wood and roses, she felt, for the first time in months, the faint whisper of belonging.

She did not know if she could ever truly love it. But she knew she would try.

And as the bird's song rose, soft and clear, she understood: this was where she was meant to be.

The Dancing in the Walls

It was rare for ordinary people like Robert and me to stay anywhere so steeped in grandeur. Yet, across a sea of silken, lush emerald lawn, my breath caught at the sight of its haughty façade. Tall spires rose high into the sky—arrogant, frosted peaks reaching for an unknown haven. Beneath them, countless windows glimmered with an air of superiority, like antique lanterns whispering invitations to a world of wonder, wildness and, perhaps, wickedness. Regal though it appeared, my instincts told me this was no mansion but a cursed castle with secrets buried deep in its dark underbelly.

I told Robert as much, murmuring my impressions. He only clasped my shoulder and gave me that look—half pity, half indulgence—reserved for someone whose poor health had, in his eyes, made them a little fanciful.

We followed the final curve of the path and stepped inside. My sleeping quarters engulfed me in a single colour: moss green. Velvety drapes cascaded from the canopy bed like an enchanted waterfall, pooling on the floor. Sheets, carpet, even the walls—all green. The effect was suffocating and strangely seductive, as though the room wished to swallow me whole.

"Come now, dear," Robert murmured. "Let's get you tucked in. It's been such a long journey for you."

I glanced at him, then back into the murky depths. Perhaps it was not so bad. Perhaps this place would be comforting, restorative. That was why I had come, after all—to rest my exhausted body.

***

Morning brought birdsong and the scent of muffins and jam. I joined Robert downstairs, but after only a few bites, my arms grew heavy and my vision blurred. The muffin tumbled from my limp grasp, landing in a scarlet smear on the immaculate wooden floor. Fatigue descended suddenly and unwelcome, like a cold, dense, leaden cloud.

With a heavy sigh, Robert helped me back upstairs. Along the way, I caught his small signs of irritation and fleeting glances of sorrow.

They hurt more than the sickness.

Days passed with me confined to bed, my mind earnestly willing but my body unable to recover from the journey. Brief, fleeting moments of normality were always swiftly stolen away.

The doctor came, muttered something about "hysteria", and left.

Robert sighed again and followed him out.

Alone, I traced the patterns on the wallpaper from the confines of my bed. The green seemed deeper now, almost alive. For the first time, I noticed shapes flickering in the shadows—small, almost human—before my silent, dark predator overtook me again, and I was forced to submit to its will.

***

One night, I was woken by a furious storm roaring above. The house shuddered, and shadows danced across the walls. The moss moved, animated by the wind's command. I buried myself under the covers, becoming part of the forest.

After the storm, the figure (for I now knew it was just one) in the wallpaper became clearer—a woman, spinning and swaying in the green jungle like a ballerina moving with her surroundings, just as I used to before this curse. I was fixated on her, my fingers enchanted as they joined her dance through the wallpaper.

***

Many days later, when Robert insisted on some fresh air, I reluctantly let him lead me outside. Blinking blearily, the flowers and colours dazzled me, but as my feet began to fail me, my thoughts drifted back to my room… to her… to the dancing.

I felt suddenly compelled to tell Robert that I needed to retreat indoors, although I was sure my legs could have carried me a little further along the path. I felt only a flicker of guilt for misleading him.

Back inside, I pressed my hands desperately against the wall, breathing deeply in relief at being reunited with my little dancer. She spun faster now, reaching for me. I tried to reach back, to connect with her, to join her physically, and a small sob escaped at my sadness for not being able to.

I began scratching at the wallpaper, willing her closeness and liberation, until crimson droplets fell from my fingertips like dying rose petals.

***

During the days that followed, Robert grew impatient with me. He could not see her, blamed me for not trying harder to heal, and his voice turned sharp.

I did not understand why he would not leave me alone. I knew what I needed to do: I had to free her. And then one day, after he phoned the doctor, he physically forced me from the green lagoon. Grabbing my arms and lifting me clear off my feet, I suddenly became a wild cat, hissing and spitting as he carried me from the room. I clawed, scratched, bit, fighting to stay with the woman's mesmerising, elegant dance.

Howling, he locked me in a new prison deemed "suitable": a small, dark blue room with tiny windows overlooking the gardens. I suppose it was meant to take away my ability to escape.

Exhausted, I collapsed onto the floor, sobbing in a chaotic heap, staring blankly at the plain blue walls. They only amplified my misery and loneliness in my new confines.

After many hours of lying, unable to move after my burst of energy, my mind began to slow.

I needed a plan.

***

Over the next week, I learnt the routine prepared for me. Robert came at precisely 8 a.m., 1 p.m. and 6 p.m. with meals. These were also my designated toilet breaks, and all empty plates were removed at the next delivery. At exactly 8 p.m., he would merrily call out, "Goodnight, darling," trying longingly to sound normal, making it clear I was to go straight to sleep.

But even that sweet relief abandoned me. My mind now raced constantly like a startled hare. I could not stop thinking of the woman dancing in the wall. She must be so terribly frightened and isolated now that I was not there to keep her company. Without me, her only chance of escape had been cruelly snatched away. I could not abandon her.

***

My plan took a few more days to form. I knew I had to be patient; my weakened, frail body could not physically challenge Robert, but my mind was still sharp. Late at night, I refrained from stacking the plates neatly for Robert to remove the following morning, as I usually did. Instead, I hurled them haphazardly across the room, being mindful to make as much noise as possible. The soup from one bowl was tipped over the bedding; the rosehip tea was poured carelessly by the door.

***

When Robert entered groggily the next morning and slipped on the tea, I smiled in delight.

"What is this awful mess?" he exclaimed tiredly. "How will you ever get better if you do not eat what I provide?"

My heart twinged at the exhausted lines etched across his face as he bent to collect the scattered cutlery and plates. The feeling lasted only a moment. I saw my chance when he pricked his finger on a smashed bowl by the bed. I darted from the room as swiftly as my feeble legs allowed.

Panting heavily, I threw myself into my lush green sanctuary and hurried to barricade the door with a chair.

Giggling, I let my legs collapse beneath me, sliding down the wall. We were reunited at last.

I pressed my face to the wallpaper and breathed in its musty scent. In my peripheral vision, she whirled, and I sighed with relief as I pressed my fingers back into their familiar patterns and traced her every move.

I could focus on nothing but her shifting dance, even as I heard Robert bashing frantically at the door.

I began to feel disoriented and disturbed. I was back with her, but she was still not free. My being here was not enough. How could it ever be enough? I resumed my scratching. There had to be a way through, a way for her to re-enter the world and dance in the light.

Every second that she spun past, I clawed at the walls more and more frantically. It was not fair for her to be trapped, forced to live in the shadows.

Crimson blood swelled and flowed from my fingers. She continued to twirl, even as she became stained by my bloody efforts. But it was futile; she remained imprisoned behind the wallpaper.

Violently, I clawed until my nails splintered, until the green swam before my eyes and suffocated my very being.

She stopped dancing.

She was staring.

I was staring.

She had my hair…

My mouth…

My eyes…

She looked so alive…

And I was no longer sure I was.

Pippinella and the Three Fairies

One unusually usual morning, Pippinella skipped merrily along the winding woodland path. The birds were singing chirpily upside down, the mushrooms were twirling topsy-turvily, and the grass sighed softly beneath her feet as though she were heavier than a ladybird's shadow. Pippinella, however, felt as light as a hiccup's dream.

Today she was going to visit her three fairy friends: Dewdrop, Sunpetal, and Willowmist. She had never been to their home before, though she had imagined it endlessly: once as a house knitted entirely from whiskers, once as a shoe that laced itself, and once as an enormous ticklish sneeze with curtains.

When at last she reached it, she gasped. The cottage was alive with contradictions. Its roof wriggled in greeting, the windows blinked with suspicion, and the door leaned down to whisper, "Do you knock, or do you knock-knock?" Pippinella giggled, which seemed to be the correct answer, for the door flung itself open in delight.

Inside, the floor rippled like porridge that could not decide whether it was hot or cold. Pippinella staggered, laughing nervously, just as the three fairies swooped upon her in a dazzling flurry of wings.

"Welcome, welcome!" sang Dewdrop.

"Or is it farewell, farewell?" asked Sunpetal.

"Both are the same if you sit long enough," added Willowmist gravely.

They hugged her until she felt quite like a loaf being kneaded, then pulled her towards a curious table that seemed to be nibbling at its own legs.

"Sit! Sit! You must be starving!" cried Willowmist.

Pippinella lowered herself onto the nearest seat, only to feel her bottom squeak indignantly. "My, your chairs are very firm."

"That is not a chair," giggled Sunpetal. "It is a hazelnut."

The nut gave a furious wiggle, tossed her into the air, and scuttled off muttering, "Guests these days! Not an ounce of respect for fine furniture!"

"Try mine!" Dewdrop cried, pushing forward a sunflower chair. "It asked to be useful, and I said, 'Be careful what you wish for.'"

Pippinella sat, but the stem shivered in exaggerated despair. The sunflower lowered her gently with a sigh, turned away, and declared mournfully, "She is too much gravity for me."

"Then the leaves!" Willowmist insisted, patting a stack that shimmered like green glass. "Neither too soft nor too hard, but exactly somewhere else."

Pippinella sat. The leaves began to drift and swirl as though they had swallowed the sky. Up, down, sideways, around—soon she was dizzy as a compass caught in a washing machine. With a yelp, she slid to the floor.

"The floor seems safest," she muttered, smoothing her skirts.

The fairies clapped their hands in delight.

"Safe is dangerous!" said Dewdrop.

"Dangerous is safe!" said Sunpetal.

"Unless it isn't," added Willowmist, nodding wisely.

Then all three leaned towards her and whispered quietly together:

"Tell us, Pippinella, when is a chair not a chair?"

Pippinella blinked. "When it has legs and runs away?"

The fairies shrieked with glee, tumbling into one another. "Correct! Incorrect! Both! Neither! You are cleverer than we thought and sillier than we hoped!"

The floor gave another pleased shiver beneath her. It was glad to be included in the riddle, even though it had not the faintest idea what the answer was.

"Quadruppley comes the nibblerly nibbles," cried Willowmist, who produced a hat of guitar keys that bowed and purred with anticipation.

"I am not sure I can eat that," gulped Pippinella with a look of disbelief, like a meadow that no longer knew how to fly.

At once, two old dishes floated forward on silver saucers, balancing like jugglers on invisible toes.

The last meal was a pie, but the crust was made of paper maps, so every bite sent her tongue wandering down rivers and over mountains until she lost track of her own mouth.

The first meal was a sandwich, yet the bread sighed like pillows, so soft that the cheese and lettuce escaped and ran laughing across the floor in a giggle of bubbles.

"Not quite right, not quite wrong!" sang the fairies, delighted. "A feast of mischief for a hungry questioner!"

"And hungry questioners make sleepy answers!" all the fairies chanted.

But before Pippinella could choose whether to laugh or pout, three shadows tiptoed in, each carrying a smirk the way one carries an umbrella.

The second bed was a clock that ticked backwards only when she looked at it, making her feel as though she had sneezed in the wrong direction of time.

The first bed was a scolding breeze, which told her she had tied her shoelaces far too merrily.

The third bed was a cracked teacup that refused to hold tea but insisted on holding grudges instead.

"Too bad to be good, too good to be bad!" chorused the fairies. "What will you do with them, Pippinella?"

The floor wriggled beneath her, curious.

Pippinella pressed her palms to her cheeks. The soup that ate itself, the sandwich that ran away, the scolding breeze, the backward clock—it all tumbled about inside her head like a sack of stationary marbles.

“I think…” she whispered, her voice quivery as a violin string, “I think it is all too much. I do not know which way is up anymore.”

The fairies drooped at once, their wings folding like wilted petals. “Too many riddles! Too many muddles! We never meant to topple your thinking so completely.”

The floor, embarrassed, stopped shivering and tried to behave like an ordinary floor, though it was not very good at it, all mismatched and higgledy-piggledy.

Pippinella gave a small, crooked smile. “Thank you for everything. It was wonderful, wonderful and strange, but I think I need to go where spoons do not drink soup, and clocks do not chase me backwards.”

She stepped towards the hush-door as it opened, soft and silvery, like a secret she was not meant to keep.

The fairies waved their curious meals and upside-down bids in farewell, their voices threading together like a sad song. “Go then, Pippinella. But promise you will remember us, even if you never quite understand us.”

She nodded, though her throat ached. And then she went back to the steady world, where everything made sense.

Only… on the quietest days, when chairs sat too still and clocks ticked too predictably, Pippinella would sigh and wish, just a little, that she could be confused again.

Uncertain Paths

Once upon a time, at the very edge of Foresty Wood, there lived a girl named Red. She shared a small, cheerful home with her mother and father, who loved her more than anything else in the whole world. Deep in the heart of the forest, in a curiously cosy little cottage, lived Red's dear grandmother. The two adored one another so dearly that one day her grandmother made a beautiful red velvet cape for her. Red treasured the gift and wore it lovingly.

Red's grandmother was very elderly, and Red never missed a day of visiting her with a basket of her favourite treats. That morning, the kitchen smelled warm and sweet as Red's mother pulled a golden sponge cake fresh from the oven and carefully cut a generous slice for Red to take with her to her grandmother.

Excited to be setting out on her travels, Red skipped blissfully down the familiar, winding path that led deep into Foresty Wood. In the branches above, the birds merrily sang their cheerful chorus, and a playful beam of sunlight danced naughtily across her nose, making her giggle. The forest felt alive with sparkle and song, and her feet seemed to know the way on their own, carrying her along as she gathered bright, beautiful flowers for her grandmother.

When she reached her favourite tree, she plucked a shining apple from its branch and smiled. "Thank you, Mr Tree," she said sweetly. "Your apples fill my heart with joy. May I take one to my granny as well?"

With a soft rustle, the tree seemed to grant its permission, and Red carefully placed a second apple in her wicker basket. But as she turned to continue on her way, she noticed something strange. The once-bright path ahead had grown dark and twisted. Red hesitated, her heart fluttering. The forest seemed different now, hushed and watchful. Still, she took a deep breath and pressed forward. The woods had never harmed her before, and her grandmother's cosy cottage was not far away.

Pad. Pad. Pad.

Red's ears pricked timidly at the soft, deliberate sound of footsteps beside her. She turned her head, peering deeply through the tangle of bushes and brambles, hoping to glimpse a friendly face. But all she saw was a deep, velvet darkness where, it seemed, the forest light dared not to tiptoe.

Pad. Pad. Pad.

Her breath caught as a solid shape emerged from the gloom—a gigantic wolf, his fur blending with the shadows, his gleaming golden eyes fixed steadily ahead. He matched her pace perfectly, his enormous paws steady and firm.

Red froze. The wolf froze. She took a careful step forward, heart hammering. The wolf strode forward, too. She stepped back; he stepped back. All the while, he stayed just within the darkness of the trees, as if the shadows themselves were concealing him, like two entities working together. He never once looked at her, but Red could feel him—every muscle alert, every step an echo of her own.

He knew her every move.

A fierce wind swept through the trees, carrying a chill that seemed to accompany the wolf, and Red shivered deep down into her roots. The woods she had known so well now felt strange and frightening.

But she refused to let fear turn her back. Determined, she pressed on, keeping a wary eye on the wolf whenever she could glimpse him through the undergrowth.

She knew wolves were unpredictable, and even when he disappeared from sight, she could not shake the feeling of sharp, golden eyes observing from the shadows.

At last, she arrived at her grandmother's cottage, and a huge sigh of relief escaped her lips. The moment her grandmother opened the old wooden door and wrapped her in a warm embrace, the dark path outside faded in her mind like a foggy day gently blown away by a soft breeze. The danger, the shadows, the strange hush of the forest, all of it melted away in the presence of her grandmother's glow of love and safety.

On the journey home, the familiar path had returned to its sun-dappled, welcoming self. Red savoured every step, her feet springing lightly over the crisp, warm leaves as they always had before.

***

Over the next few days, Red wandered through the woods with a heart full of joy and contentment. She savoured fresh, delicious apples, exchanged quiet greetings with the friendlier trees (though most preferred the solitude to ponder the stories of the seasons), and breathed in the heady fragrance of flowers that spilled across the winding path.

The wolf became little more than a shadowy echo in her memory, a creature she sometimes wondered if she had only dreamed. Yet occasionally, when a rustle stirred in the undergrowth or a flicker of golden eyes caught the corner of her vision, she felt a shiver run down her spine. Perhaps he was still there, somewhere in the forest, watching and waiting, but never close enough to startle her again.

Then, on one seemingly calm morning, the path turned suddenly gloomy again when she was halfway to her grandmother's. Her heart sank when she heard it once more soft, deliberate, unmistakable: Pad. Pad. Pad.

She had only paused for a second when suddenly the wolf lunged toward her, and a storm of hail crashed down like a barrage of icy bullets. Panic surged through Red, and she ran. She darted through the trees and brambles, the thorns tearing at her cape and scratching her skin, drawing drops of blood that fell like tiny, extinguished crimson stars along the forest floor.

Crying out, a huge branch slammed into her stomach, wrenching her off her feet and leaving her gasping for breath. The relentless Pad. Pad. Pad. followed close behind. Shaking, she forced herself to her feet and stumbled the last few steps, tumbling against her grandmother's door with a thud.

Startled, she looked up at her grandmother's welcoming face as the door swung open.

“Grandma!” gasped Red. “I’ve had the most awful journey. Look!”

But as she looked down and presented her bloodied arms, she saw that not one mark marred them. Not one spot of blood. Not one scratch.

“Come in, dear,” smiled her grandmother softly. “We’ll get you some nice apple juice that I’ve just made.”

Afterwards, she stumbled back through the woods, disoriented and confused. All the while, she knew the wolf was still there—watching, silent and unseen, like a shadow of light that clung to her, a velvet shroud lingering just beyond sight.

All that night, Red wished with all her being that the wolf would leave her alone, that she could visit her grandmother in tranquillity again.

Yet the pattern continued relentlessly, and the wolf began appearing more and more. Some days she skipped along the sunlit path, the warmth of the light lifting her spirits, while on other days the forest seemed to close in around her, thick darkness pressing from every side, suffocating her in a haze of fog and unease.

However, whatever path was presented to her each morning, she now knew with complete certainty that the wolf was always there, watching, waiting. It had become like a second ominous shadow to her, one that she could not shake off. And when she listened closely, she could always hear it—the soft, deliberate Pad. Pad. Pad. of his paws trailing her through the trees.

On the days when the harder stretches of the path presented themselves, she stayed resolute, pushing forward despite the fear gnawing at her. She had faced these woods before and made it through, and she knew she would again as long as she refused to give up.

***

That was until one particular day, when the darkness encapsulated all light, the winds howled hauntingly, and the trees thrashed furiously against their very roots. Red knew she didn't have far to go now, but she also knew the wolf was observing close to the path. She was a butterfly tangled in the deadly jaws of silence.

Just as she thought she saw a glimpse of her grandmother's cottage, the wolf pounced: a predatory curse uncoiled. With a startled scream, she reeled backwards into the unforgiving, prickly bush that curled round the path like an insidious snake. As she crumbled into the dense heap of thorns and spikes, Red gave a sharp cry of anguish and lay numbly where she landed.

Although dazed, she still silently felt the wolf slowly approaching. Pad. Pad. Pad. Urgently, her heart hammered in her chest like a hummingbird hopelessly trying to escape its confines.

She squeezed her eyes shut and wished with every fibre of her being to vanish and be safe and warm at her grandmother's.

The minutes slowed, and after what seemed like an eternity, she felt the wolf's humid breath on her face and its sharp claws press steadily into her arm.

Time stilled.

Petrified, Red did not move.

Neither did the wolf.

Painstakingly, she eventually summoned the courage to blink open her eyes. The wolf lay close, studying her with its huge, golden eyes. But there was no aggression, only an indifferent, measured awareness.

Breathing a tired sigh of exhaustion and pain, Red carefully inched her fingers towards the wolf's paw, as though they were being pulled by invisible strings.

She realised something she had never seen before.

"I am what I am… and you are what you are," she whispered into the cold, heavy air.

The wolf gazed at her, and as her fingers touched the fur, she felt it breathe beneath her touch. Fear washed over her, familiar and raw, but she refused to flinch. She knew the wolf would always follow her, watching, waiting, unyielding.

Staring up at the blackened sky, the rain began to fall heavily across her face.

Tears traced silver rivers along her cheeks, and she gently squeezed the wolf's paw.

The truth terrified her.

They were two stitched into one.

And there was no way the stitching could be undone.

The House of Honeyed Lies

One dull autumn evening, Elion and Merlina were cast out from their family abode into the bleak, dense forest, their stomachs hollow and their limbs weak with the secret sicknesses they carried. For though they looked like any other child, both bore afflictions that raged within: Elion with a heaviness that made his legs ache with each step, and Merlina with pains that came like a sudden blaze, igniting from within when she least expected them.

Their parents had loved them fiercely, but grief had worn them thin. For however hard they tried, they could not find any cures or answers—only a heavy, grinding boulder of despair that grew denser and denser by the day, until it was too great to bear. And so, with heavy hearts and stifled sobs, they sent their children out into the world, hoping they would be able to find the comfort that they had been unable to provide for them.

The children, seeing their parents' misery and feeling the deep yearning for a day when they might be free of their ailments, knew they had no choice but to follow their parents' orders. So, they wandered slowly, trembling and stumbling, in the forest of silent sentinels.

With every step, their bodies screamed in protest within the murky, endless abyss of trees, where shadows slithered after them and distant howls of unseen creatures reverberated through the leafy labyrinth.

Still, they pressed on, driven by determination and the fragile hope that freedom might lie beyond their pain and exhaustion.

***

Days bled into one another along the arduous path. At times, their bodies crumpled into heavy heaps upon the forest floor, yet sleep refused to claim them. In that maze of whispers, even the darkness itself seemed alive, breathing against their skin and murmuring constant threats into their ears.

***

Eventually, after many weary and woeful weeks, they were relieved to find a small house made of sugar and spice, nestled in the depths of the forest. Its roof was tiled with bright red lollipops, its windows were glazed with warm, gooey honey, and the welcoming door was pieced together with a thousand multicoloured jellybeans.

Fumbling forward, they were greeted by a kindly-looking woman who smiled as sweetly as her pretty home.

"Come inside," she beckoned, her voice low and welcoming, with a small glint in her eyes. "I see the storm in your bones; I know the trembling in your limbs. I can cure what others do not see. Here you shall eat and rest, and your pain will fade like a forgotten fog in the morning."

Elion, shaking with frailty and longing, and Merlina, trembling weakly and yearning for the woman's words to be true, both stepped cautiously into her house, where the air wrapped them in a warm, caring cuddle.

All around them lay feasts for their weary eyes to devour, while the sugary perfume of confectionery drifted through the air like golden sunlight wrapping them in warmth. The walls oozed with chunks of creamy white chocolate; candyfloss curtains bounced with playful invitation; and the floor, patched merrily with jelly babies, put a gentle spring in every step. Chairs of pillowy marshmallows waited, soft, supportive, and slightly squeaky, while at the very heart of the room stood a tremendous table, crowned with glittering domes of delectable delights.

***

For the first time in a long time, their bodies grew quiet, their pain softened, and their minds felt the tiny, forgotten nudge of hope.

The children relished the constant feeling of fullness and contentment, as the kind and gentle woman provided all that they needed and desired over the next few days.

"Do not worry, my sweets," she would often coo to them as she stroked their hair. "I am here to make you better. Each bite, each sip, each sleep, brings you closer to the cure. And when you leave, you shall feel a lightness that you could never have imagined for yourselves."

***

Even though they felt the comfort of warmth and fullness that they had not known before, they began to realise that every time they ate, every time they drank, and every time they slept in their snug, fudge-made beds, the house itself drew tighter and tighter around them, almost inconspicuously at first. The white chocolate walls leaned closer. The candy windows wept sticky tears. The honey-glass panes caught their reflections and grinned. It was subtly trapping them in its sickly-sweet cocoon, as though it meant to keep them there forever.

They also began to accept that, although all their needs were met and their hearts were filled with hope, their ailments stubbornly persisted. Elion's legs still grew heavy and leaden until at times he was unable to walk, and Merlina often cried out with the sudden pain that engulfed her limbs both during the day and in the night.

***

They now craved the familiar, loving presence of their parents.

When they tried politely to take their leave, the woman smiled gracefully and glided across the rows of intertwined jelly babies to block their path to the door. "Not yet, my little ones. You are not fully healed yet. Don't you want to get better?"

They did. Desperately.

***

Days fluttered into weeks, and the woman continued to feed and water them, promising that the next draught, the next potion, the next enchanted morsel would make them well. That it was all working how it was supposed to.

And although wellness never came, the tiny bubble of hope kept relentlessly nudging delicately within them.

They wretchedly wanted to return home, but the dream of health was too wonderful to give up on.

***

As the weeks drifted past, if anything, their sicknesses became worse. Elion's step grew heavier and heavier until his feet felt nailed to the floor, and Merlina's pains caused her breath to become fainter and fainter until it was too thin to carry her across the room.

They were trapped. Trapped in their bodies. Trapped in this house of honeyed lies, as the woman's voice became a constant hum in their heads, promising relief that would never come.

The forest outside faded.

Time faded.

And so, the house of sugar and spice clasped them tight, its sweetness turning to poison. It held them close, whispering its false promises as it swallowed them whole, its caramel curses seeping in and sticking tightly to their bones.

They understood, at last. The last spark of hope was gone… and they would never leave.

The Lady in the Mirror

In a bustling village of cosy cottages and flowing fields, there lived a young woman called Maerwyn. Her striking beauty instantly drew people to her like moths to a flame. Her skin glowed like morning sunlight spilling gently across the dewy meadows around the village. Her perfect gait was unbroken, and she glided like an angel. Her smile brightened everything it touched, unlocking a blossoming joy in all who met her.

People could not help but envy this serene picture of perfection.

Yet hidden beneath that image lay a trial and torment Maerwyn never voiced aloud. It was a weakness that gnawed insidiously at her bones, a trembling that haunted her in the secret hours of darkness, and a deep-rooted weariness that clung to her frame like a merciless shadow.

She lived with a constant dread that thudded repetitively and relentlessly beneath every thought, every moment, every word—the dread that the world would uncover the truth behind her perfection and see her for who she truly was. For back then, perfection was viewed as a prize beyond all others and a window into one's very soul, while illness was seen as a sin carried unceasingly by it. And so Maerwyn drifted through life, admired deeply by all, yet living in a ceaseless, lonely state of isolation.

***

It was after many long, exhausting years of bearing these secret struggles that she discovered the mirror.

She was visiting her elderly grandmother one sunny afternoon, who asked her to fetch a book from upstairs. Her grandmother was frail and never ventured beyond the downstairs living rooms. But as Maerwyn advanced upstairs and into her grandmother's former bedroom, she heard a strange sound drifting from somewhere above. It was not particularly abrasive, more like a soft sigh carried through the house by a gentle breeze. Yet as Maerwyn searched for the book, it grew louder, more insistent, demanding to be noticed.

Drifting curiously into the hallway and then into the room at the back of the house, she noticed a tiny, mismatched staircase leading upwards that had never caught her attention before.

Listening closely, the sound persisted, even seeming to carry her name in its now impatient exhalations.

She stepped cautiously into the abandoned attic, where cobwebs hung like ghostly laces, and her eyes were drawn to a vast, magnificent mirror leaning innocently against a dust-lined wall.

Her breath caught in her throat, and the sounds ceased as suddenly as death.

Creeping closer, drawn forward by an unseen hand, she stopped quietly before the wondrous glass framed in deep oak wood. It was intricately carved with spectacular symbols that seemed to crawl outward, like spider legs searching for their prey.

As Maerwyn traced them lightly with her fingers, her ears pricked as the soft sigh returned, encompassing her in its breathy resonance:

"Bestow on me what you desire to conceal, and I shall bury it for you within me. Let me wear your weaknesses, and you will walk through the world unmarred."

Maerwyn, desperate to continue blending harmoniously with the society around her (something which was becoming harder and harder to achieve), pressed her hands against the cold glass and murmured her consent.

Immediately, a biting blade cut through her as the mirror greedily drank in her pain and torment. She cried out in shock and slammed her eyes shut against the sudden onslaught, but when she blinked them blearily open, she realised her body felt light and carefree. For the first time in years, she felt her frame hum with a sense of peace and contentment. It was a sensation she had almost forgotten until that moment.

Dancing delightedly down the stairs, she plucked the book from the bookcase, swirled down to her grandmother with it, kissed her on the forehead, and fluttered out into a new world.

A world she had never thought she would experience again, and it was wonderful.

***

From that day, no pains or weaknesses afflicted her, and no marks of exhaustion marred her beauty. She flitted blissfully through her days and nights, to lunches, parties, and musicals. Everywhere she went, she carried an illumination of enchantment that everyone idolised. And for the first time, it was not a façade.

She was free. She was no longer a prisoner to her own body.

However, nothing is ever destroyed, only hidden, like echoes lingering long after the storm has passed. The mirror remembered, and the mirror bore the truth.

It began to twist, to distort. A velvet darkness descended over it, relentless and merciless. No one saw the changes, like roots shifting beneath frozen ground, hidden away in the attic. But sometimes it moaned, strained, withered.

A moan that prickled at Maerwyn's ears, and a persistent tug that was easily ignored at first.

***

The years passed in a flutter of song and sunlight. Although others wrinkled with age and ailment, Maerwyn remained untouched. She remained a perfect portrait of beauty and youth.

Yet she began to perceive a strange heaviness about her. It was not physical as before, but more as though part of her shadow was missing, as if it had been slowly eroding away. It was indescribable but unsettling, and it lingered there just out of sight as others began to whisper words of suspicion.

As this continued, the mirror in the attic grew old and impatient. It was no longer willing to be ignored. It became a constant, fragile pull of an invisible string, which left Maerwyn strained and, in quiet moments, as though she were half-phantom, half-human.

It became a drumbeat that echoed in an empty room, one that settled in Maerwyn's mind, low and persistent.

A drumbeat that grew sharper and harsher…

***

Eventually, Maerwyn gave way to the beat, the thread that tugged her back.

She ascended for a second time to the attic and felt tears fall like raindrops as her eyes met her broken reflection in the mirror. Her true form stared back: an abandoned entity, shattered and alone. Her eyes were hollow, her skin deathly pale, her limbs shook uncontrollably, and exhaustion wrapped around her like a spider's web.

She had so desired to banish this truth, to hide from it forever…

In fear, she hurriedly snatched a shard of wood from the floor and struck it deeply, painfully, into the centre of the mirror. She stared as the spider's tentacles cracked throughout, and the glass shattered around her feet like frozen, fragmented lightning.

She doubled over as years of fatigue, weakness, and agony crashed through her, and she leaned heavily on her knees, trying to catch her breath as she blinked exhaustedly down at the shattered stars.

Reflected in those stars, she saw herself, her true self, standing where she was.

She had expected to break like the mirror, but she did not.

Shocked, she managed to rise. The flawless figure was obliterated. Her step was unsteady, her body exhausted, her limbs heavy, but her eyes now carried a new light and strength.

The mirror was no more; her truth was her own; her shadow was her own.

In that moment, she finally realised that strength came from acceptance, and she returned to the world imperfect, but human.

A human who no longer hid from her own true beauty.

The Monsters Within

Many years ago, at the very edge of a wide, whispering forest, a young woman named Freya lived in a castle filled with roses. She was kind, curious, and thoughtful, but within those quiet walls also resided something else—a presence that did not have a name.

Freya called it the Beast.

And it haunted her every waking moment.

It prowled hungrily in the shadows, breathed softly against her hair, and poured whispered warnings into her ears that made her hands tremble and her chest tighten.

Whenever she thought of stepping beyond the gates of her familiar abode, the Beast's voice would rise, dark and certain: "What if you fail? What if you are not enough?" It would roar deafeningly: "You'll never be enough!" if she lingered too long by the door.

And Freya would retreat back into herself, accepting that the world outside was not for her.

When visitors came, no one saw the Beast stalking in the background. They saw only Freya's sweet smile and her careful politeness. But Freya always felt it—growing and growling in the shadows with her, prowling unforgivingly through her thoughts. It questioned every hesitation, every answer, every decision. It kept her from travelling, from speaking the words that trembled on her lips, from dancing under the stars as she so longed to do.

And deep down, Freya believed its words, for she carried an unknown ailment that set her apart from others in the town. She was different. "Wrong," the Beast whispered to her in the middle of the night.

Still, she tried. Many mornings, she made herself stand by the door, her heart fluttering, her fingers trembling as they longed to reach out and grasp the handle. But each time she did, the Beast would tighten its grip around her chest until she felt as though she was suffocating, with no choice but to let the Beast win again.

Dejectedly, she would lovingly stroke the crimson rose in the centre of the hall, a gift from her grandmother, and remember her grandmother's words: "Keep the light burning here, as you keep it burning in your heart."

But the Beast always returned, snarling violently from the edges: "What happens if you fall? Who will help you? What happens when no one cares?"

And Freya would retreat into the quietness of the castle. Safe. Secure. But alone and afraid.

***

As the seasons passed, her grandmother's red rose began to lose its petals, one by one, bleeding across the floor like hours slipping through an hourglass. Freya found herself lingering at her window more and more, staring at the outside world. So close. So impossibly far away.

"Don't," the Beast hissed. "It's not safe."

As was always the way, she remained.

But beyond the doors, a single red rose bloomed in the wild grass, bright, defiant, beautiful as though calling her name. It haunted her dreams, this other rose, begging her to come and pluck it. The more it bloomed, the louder the Beast became, howling its warnings: that she was not enough, that people would see her weakness, that she would break if she tried.

***

One morning, Freya woke to find the last petal had fallen sadly from the rose in the hall. It lay on the cold, stone floor like a drop of blood, and the light of the castle seemed dimmer, as though it had died with it.

She knew she had to leave to escape this prison, just for a moment, to bring light back into the castle, and maybe back into her own soul.

Her heart began to pound. The air pressed heavily around her. She could not breathe. But she knew it was time.

And then, in the choking silence, she heard something new, not the Beast's snarl, but its whimper.

Its quiet, frightened whimper.

Freya froze.

Stunned.

Her eyes widened in surprise. She finally understood. The Beast was not separate from her. It was hers—her fear, her grief, her doubt—huddled in the shadows because it thought it was keeping her safe.

She took a slow, trembling breath.

"Come with me," she whispered, now understanding that it was the Beast that needed to be looked after. To be cared for.

The Beast was silent.

Watchful.

Moving…

Perhaps unmoving…

With her heart hammering, Freya stepped forward and placed her hand tentatively on the door handle…

Tower of the Sleeplessness

The storm rages furiously.

Stones shiver in shock.

Rain hammers down upon the quiet, sentinel earth.

Winds slam tempestuously through the gates, howling in a language she can almost comprehend.

At the entrance, she stands silent, drenched and quivering.

A forgotten ghost in a dull, grey gown.

From beyond the door, egotistical eyes follow her every tremble.

Too many watchful eyes. Too sharp. Too piercing.

The queen opens the exit.

She takes her hand. It twists and turns like a sinuous snake.

Staircases fall and rise.

They spiral out and in upon themselves.

Long, hollow corridors wrap and warp.

Too narrow. Too wide. Too dark. Too bright.

She staggers.

She stumbles.

She misses a step.

Her mind distorts.

Her body folds in pleats and creases.

Nausea washes over her like a tsunami.

No one notices.

No one cares.

After thousands of years, they reach her prison for the night.

A cold chamber.

A bitter, bossy bed.

No, a hysterical hillside.

No. No. A monstrous mountain.

Twenty mattresses collapsing into eternity.

Twenty mattresses, twenty quilts, twenty pillow coffins.

Alive.

And hiding, slyly, beneath it all, one petite pea.

Minuscule.

Brutal.

Smiling.

The walls dance.

The rain laughs.

The wind giggles.

The girl quivers.

From the storm. From the petite pea. From her own soul.

A monstrous mountain spitting her out…

Fragmented.

It swells and swallows her whole.

A silent scream.

A pea.

Minuscule.

Brutal.

Smiling.

Sleep, they order. Wake, they suggest.

The words stab like blunted beetles. The words echo backwards into the hellish helix.

Covers nibble and devour suffocating skin.

Pillows bend and flatten fragile frames.

The darkness engulfs, digests, smothers.

Alive.

The pea.

Minuscule.

Brutal.

Smiling.

Knives comfort and contort.

Beneath her skin. Inside her skull.

Sound splinters.

Lights explode. Implode?

Extinguishing and igniting.

Sleep?

Disintegrates into an abyss.

Time shortens, stretches, and scrutinises.

Its jagged shards seek and surrender.

She hangs.

She falls.

She clings.

The pea.

Minuscule.

Brutal.

Smiling.

Dusk peeks its head out. Dawn peers around the corner.

Glass shatters over her. Around her. Inside her.

Broken eyes.

Severed skin.

Snapped soul.

"I…did not sleep," she whispers. "There was something under the bed."

The Trail of Fog and Fogginess

On one particularly bright morning, Faye was skipping through her forest, as she happened to do every day. The forest brimmed with wonder, joy, and contentment, and she loved nothing more than singing greetings to the birds, collecting faithful flowers, and eating bumbling berries.

Swinging her wicker basket, she closed her eyes as the forest's breath, earthy pine and soft moss, unfolded around her like a secret meant only for her. Surrounded by serenity, she was about to coo to the pigeons when the lush green, emerald ocean was suddenly engulfed by a blanket of fog as the trees folded in upon themselves.

A pygmy goat popped up from the bushes.

"To pass through the fog, you must answer my riddles," sang the goat, plonking a bright purple top hat on his head.

Befuddled, Faye found the fog had wriggled into her ears, stuffing her head with cotton wool. Thoughts wobbled and drifted away like leaves in a stream, and she could barely hold on to a single coherent idea.

"I…I don't like mushrooms…spoons…no, riddles!" she stammered, shaking her head as she tried to clear the haze.

"You can put me inside a drawer and outside a moon at the same time; I taste like Tuesday but sound like a folded map. What am I?" brightly chirped the pygmy goat.

Faye blinked blankly, her thoughts slipping further away into the distance.

"I climb ladders made of pancakes and apologise to the wallpaper every spring. I have three elbows and one polite hat. Who am I?"

Faye stared, bewildered. Her head felt heavy, as though it were wading through honey.

"I wear the smell of old books and ride a bicycle that only works on rainy Wednesdays. Sometimes I count socks backwards. What am I?"

Faye furrowed her brows, trying intently to make sense of these words, but they tugged and teased each other in a mischievous game.

"I once traded my shadow for a paperclip, and now I owe a library three confessions. My shoes are made of yesterday. What am I?"

Faye tilted her head in confusion, the words twisting and twirling in her mind before she had a chance to hold them still.

"I am a conversation you can carry between two pencils. I apologise in advance for the weather. What am I?"

Faye shrugged helplessly, unable to navigate the labyrinth her mind had naughtily become.

But the pygmy goat was growing impatient.

"At least try to riddle a riddle with me?" cried the goat as he stomped his happy hoof on the forest floor.

"I can't!" sobbed Faye as the mist coiled around her. "I don't understand…why…you're here…in the lush…green…mountain…forest…urghhh…"

After a moment's consideration, the pygmy goat simply swapped his purple top hat for a blue one and continued his riddles.

"I am the polite echo that returns only questions nobody asked. I keep a calendar of fingerprints. What am I?"

"Stop it! I don't know! I can't think!" Faye exclaimed, curling into herself. "This…is not…happy… buttercup…ummm…question mark…bad!"

"Yes!" cheered the pygmy goat. "It is a question mark. You may continue on your path."

And with a simple pop, the pygmy goat vanished, and the fog dissolved into a dream.

The forest's colours returned; Faye's thoughts became her own again.

Shaking away the last whispers, Faye carried on her way, her song soft and thoughtful. She knew that, at the back of her mind, the forest's fog lingered, ready to curl around her thoughts like a mischievous ribbon once more.

The Never-Ending Dance

Between the mountains, by a stream of silver, there lived a girl named Lilienne. She was bright and beautiful, yet she lived in poverty, her days filled with hunger and hardship. In her heart, she carried a single dream — to dance. To dance as if the world itself were her stage, to feel wild freedom bloom through her body, the kind that comes only from the art of movement.

But her family's struggles made such dreams impossible. They could not afford dance lessons, nor could they buy the dazzling red shoes she admired each time she passed Old Maggie's Shoe Shop. Still, she would linger at the window whenever she walked by, pressing her nose to the glass as her breath fogged it, longing for what she saw beyond.

For dreams have a way of surviving, and she never let the hope she held so tightly fly away.

***

Years passed, and her family's struggles only deepened. Her father grew older, his back more bent, and her mother grew weary with the burden and sadness of keeping her family fed.

***

Then, one day, word arrived that a distant relative had died. It was a sad and sudden loss, but with it came an inheritance that finally lifted the family's troubles.

Although saddened by the news, Lilienne could not help her thoughts from flying at once to the window of Old Maggie's shop, and she felt the hope inside her swell and purr.

***

A week later, her father came home from work with a spring in his step and a joy that spilt from him like sunlight.

"Lilienne! I have something very special for you," he called cheerfully, holding out a box wrapped in bright red paper, barely able to contain the excitement bubbling inside him.

Lilienne's breath caught in her throat at the sight. She carefully took the box from him and tore it open with trembling hands.

There they were. The red shoes. Her red shoes.

Tears blurred her vision as she thanked her father and slipped them onto her feet. They were even more beautiful up close, and she vowed then and there never to take them off.

***

The very next day, she attended her first dance class in the village. And from that moment, she blossomed. She worked with radiant, fierce determination, and soon she was performing on stage, her heart soaring like a skylark as the red shoes carried her magnificently across every floor they touched.

***

Everywhere she danced, joy followed. Audiences whispered, "What dazzling shoes! You sparkle in them. You must never take them off." At this, Lilienne smiled sweetly, her heart echoing with the triumph of her own spirit.

***

However, as time passed, Lilienne began to feel a heaviness creep into her limbs. At first, it was barely noticeable, but each leap grew harder and harder. Each spin became more and more dizzying. Yet she could not stop. She had to keep dancing for herself, for her family, and for the crowds who adored her.

So, she danced.

And danced.

And danced, as the shoes began to change imperceptibly. Their crimson glow deepened, and they often gleamed like a fierce fire beneath the stage lights.

They gripped Lilienne's feet tighter and tighter until they became unbearably painful to wear. At last, the agony consumed her, and regretfully, she felt she had no choice but to remove them.

Yet when she tugged at them, they would not move. They clung harshly to her like ivy to stone, and as she pulled, their grip only tightened until her fingers bled from the desperation of seeking release from the pain.

But her attempts were futile. The shoes had become part of her. Their soles were her soles; their skin was her skin.

***

From that night onward, they danced her. Her body ached, her toes bled, her ankles cracked. But still she danced. Whenever the music began, the shoes answered their master and moved of their own will, dragging her despondently with them.

***

"Please," she begged brokenly, "let me rest."

But the shoes did not listen. They only obeyed the melody.

The audiences never saw her torment. They only saw the beauty. They clapped and cheered as she spun and leapt, never knowing that every smile cost her another agonising turn, that every applause was another shattering leap.

***

Night blurred into day, and day into night. She danced and danced, unable to stop, unable even to sleep.

Until one night, she looked down and saw that her feet were no longer hers at all. The shoes had hungrily consumed them, glowing like a living flame.

***

In that moment, she understood.

She would dance forever. Until nothing remained of her but an empty shell. An empty shell moved by relentless, resplendent, red shoes.

The Girl Who Refused to Drink the Moon

Long, long ago, there was a miller's daughter named Thessaly, who was locked in a tower stuffed with so much wool that sheep in distant kingdoms were wandering about chilly and embarrassed.

Her job? To weave it all into a never-ending stream of blankets and coats, because her father had somehow managed to lose a fortune betting on snail races.

"I expect to find one hundred pink and yellow blankets by morning," the king declared pompously, puffing out his chest so far he nearly toppled over. "Each must be softer than cloud feathers, shinier than a smug swan, and perfectly identical or your father shall pay!"

Thessaly stared at the mountain of wool, then at her own two hands, which were more noodle than muscle.

"Well, that's absurd," she said flatly. "My little arms, foggy brain, and weary limbs cannot do that."

The courtiers gasped. No one had ever told the king his demands were absurd, at least not anyone who still had their head attached.

"Do not trick us, little girl!" one sniffed once the shock had flown away. "You look perfectly fine."

"We all get tired sometimes!" said another. "And if you think yourself unwell, perhaps you should simply think yourself well."

"Yes! Wellness and strength are a mindset!" shouted a third. "My cousin's aunt's fish once had this very problem. It improved after a little talk and a squeeze of lemon. Have you tried that?"

"Oh yes," Thessaly said, "I try it every morning whilst juggling hedgehogs. Makes no difference."

Scandalised, the courtiers fled, leaving Thessaly alone with the impossible task.

***

That night, just as she was about to use the wool pile as a very soft grave, a pixie-like boy popped into the room, glitter trailing behind him like breadcrumbs.

"I shall make the blankets for you," he said solemnly. "But you must prove your willingness to get better. Go into the woods, dance round five purple mushrooms, and kiss an orange frog precisely when the breeze makes the grass sing."

"That's nonsense," Thessaly said.

"Yes," he admitted cheerfully. "But it's very magical nonsense."

"Well, fine," she said with a shrug, for the alternative was weaving until she turned into a blanket herself.

***

She trudged into the forest, muttering the entire way, stomped around five mushrooms (she did not dance, she stomped), and kissed an extremely startled orange frog who then demanded she buy him dinner first.

***

By dawn, one hundred blankets were stacked neatly in her chamber.

The king returned, bellowing, "Splendid! Tonight, I want two hundred neon green coats!"

"You want two hundred coats; I want a castle made of cake. We can't all have what we want," Thessaly snapped, but no one listened.

***

Again, the pixie appeared that night. "You must hop on one leg whilst reciting the alphabet backwards, balancing a teacup of rainbow jellybeans on your head."

Thessaly gave him a long, slow look. "If I do that, will you also knit the king an ego cosy to keep it warm?"

But she did it anyway: badly. She spilt three jellybeans, tripped over the letter M, and insulted the alphabet twice, yet somehow, the coats appeared.

***

The next day, the king demanded both: one hundred pink and yellow blankets and two hundred neon green coats.

***

That night, the pixie boy returned, looking faintly annoyed. "You're not trying hard enough to get better! Now, you'll have to eat one hundred berries, ride a blue dragon, and drink the moonlight!"

Thessaly laughed in his face. "You know what? No. I'm not eating a single berry, and if the moon wants to be drunk, it can drink me."

The pixie blinked. "But…"

"But nothing." Thessaly crossed her arms. "You want to help? Fine. But I am done jumping through magical hoops like some tired circus penguin."

And she did not do a single thing he asked. She just went to bed.

***

The next morning, the blankets and coats were waiting anyway because the pixie, thoroughly scandalised by her audacity, had made them out of affectionate spite.

The king was overjoyed, her father's debts were forgiven, and Thessaly simply walked out of the tower before anyone could dream up a new demand.

She left behind the wool, the king, the courtiers, and even the pixie (who was still sputtering indignantly).

Smiling, she strode into the forest, free at last, and though she never drank moonlight, she did vow to live happily ever after and never listen to any such nonsense again.

Once upon a time

There was a girl who needed to sleep a lot

So, she did

And she lived happily ever after.

The End

About the Author

Heather is a storyteller who believes that even in the hardest chapters, there's room for wonder. Blending the magic of fairy tales with the truth of chronic illness, she writes to remind readers that every journey, no matter how heavy, holds hope, courage, and a touch of light. When she's not writing, you can usually find her daydreaming about new worlds and dragons, finding quiet moments of peace in her own, and connecting with readers who believe that even the darkest stories can hold a little light.

Living with MS has shaped my life and my stories. All proceeds from this book go to The MS Society, The MS Trust and Shift. MS, to help support others on their journeys with MS.